A catalogue record for this book is available from the British Library

Published by Ladybird Books Ltd
80 Strand London WC2R 0RL
A Penguin Company

4 6 8 10 9 7 5 3

© Ladybird Books Ltd MMVI

ISBN-13: 978-1-84422-956-7
ISBN-10: 1-84422-956-4

Printed in Italy

Fast
Fire Engine

written by Jillian Harker
illustrated by Ruth Galloway

All over town, the morning traffic
is filling the streets with noise.
Inside the fire station everything
is calm and quiet. Behind the
huge doors, a red fire engine
stands waiting. The paintwork is
polished. The brass is shining.
If there's trouble anywhere,
Fast Fire Engine is ready to rush
to the rescue.

Brrrrring! The sound of the alarm bell breaks the silence. Fast Fire Engine jumps to life, as Fireman Frank leaps on board.

Swooosh! Whoosh! The rest of the crew slide down the pole and slip into their uniforms. Jump on quickly, everyone! Fast Fire Engine starts for the exit.

Nee-naw! Now it's Fast Fire Engine who is filling the streets with noise. The siren sounds a warning. Make way, make way! There's no time to waste when someone needs help.

Heads turn as Fast Fire Engine flashes past. Cars and traffic move out of the way at the crossroads. Thanks, everyone!

Fast Fire Engine heads straight out of town and along the country roads.

Suddenly, Fast Fire Engine stops by a gate. Get it open quickly, Fireman Frank. Head straight for that tall tree over there.

Whoops! Surely that hot air balloon didn't mean to land there?

Four worried faces look down at Fast Fire Engine. Hang on! You'll soon be back on the ground.

At the press of a button, Fast Fire Engine raises a long ladder towards the people stuck in the tree. Hold it steady. Slowly does it. One at a time onto the platform and down they come. That's one rescue sorted out!

As Fast Fire Engine sets off back to town, black smoke starts to pour into the sky over Warner's Farm. That doesn't look right at all. Better go and investigate.

Poor Farmer Warner! The haystack is on fire. Thank goodness Fast Fire Engine was nearby. Don't worry, Farmer Warner! The fire will soon be under control.

Fast Fire Engine sets to work at once. Roll out the hoses. Attach them to the water main. Don't forget the air tanks, Fireman Frank, for the men working nearest to the fire. Into position, everyone! Turn on the hoses! Farmer Warner is looking much happier now that Fast Fire Engine is taking care of everything.

Fast Fire Engine keeps pumping water onto the fire. Fireman Frank aims one of the hoses to damp down the barn roof, in case any sparks fly in that direction. Thank goodness, the flames have gone out.

Mrs Warner offers the firefighters a cup of tea. Well done, Fast Fire Engine!

Fast Fire Engine gets back to the station at last. But not for long. *Brrrrring!* There goes that alarm bell again! There's no time to lose – a pipe has burst and water is pouring through the ceiling.

What a mess! Quick, on with the pumps! Fast Fire Engine will soon have everything cleaned up.

Then there's a very special call
for help. Fast Fire Engine is
needed over at the zoo. What
were the directions? Through the
gates, past the penguin pool…

right at the lion's den, left at the rhinoceros paddock. There doesn't seem to be any sign of a fire.

Well, Fast Fire Engine does get some strange jobs to do. What could Vet Victor want a ladder for?

No wonder he couldn't manage this job on his own. Poor Gerry Giraffe has toothache! Don't worry. Only a few more minutes and that will be sorted out. It's great to be able to help. It's all in a day's work for Fast Fire Engine.